We Love the Seaside

Copyright © QED Publishing 2007

First published in the UK in 2007 by
QED Publishing
A Quarto Group company
226 City Road
London EC1V 2TT
www.qed-publishing.co.uk

A catalogue record for this book is
available from the British Library.

ISBN 978 1 84538 670 2

Written by Kate Tym
Edited by Clare Weaver
Designed by Alix Wood
Illustrated by Jana Christy
Consultancy by Anne Faundez

Publisher Steve Evans
Creative Director Zeta Davies
Senior Editor Hannah Ray

Printed and bound in China

We Love the Seaside

Kate Tym

Illustrated by Jana Christy

QED Publishing

We wake up in the morning
And it's a sunny day,
Mummy grabs the cool box
And we know just what she'll say:

"Get your gear together kids,
Cossies, towels and rubber rings,
Buckets, spades and sunhats
And all your seaside things."

We take sandwiches and olives,
Crisps and apple juice,
Sun cream and flip-flops
And Billy's squeaky moose.

We take a lilo and umbrella,
Bananas and a cake,
A blanket and some sausages
And a new red plastic rake.

We take nappies and a milky bottle,
A buggy for our Billy,
Shorts for when it's sunny
And tops for when it's chilly.

There's Mum and Dad up front,
In the middle, Bill and Molly,
Then Stan and Ella in the back
With Ella's favourite dolly.

We sing songs and eat some biscuits
And Molly plays I-Spy,
And Stan starts bugging Ella
And even makes her cry.

We feel all hot and bothered,
Sticky, bored and rotten,
But when we get to the seaside
All of that's forgotten.

We pile out of the car
And race across the sand,
Ella, Stan and Molly,
Holding Billy by the hand.

We dig moats and make sandcastles,
Which we decorate with shells.
We find limpets and a starfish
And an old dead crab that smells.

Stan and Molly go swimming,
Splashing madly in the water,

While Daddy plays 'jump-wave'
With his younger son and daughter.

We find rock pools and seaweed,
Razor shells and winkles,
And Billy takes his nappy off
For outside sandy tinkles.

We play bat-and-ball and frisbee,
Catch, and have a race,
Then bury Daddy in the sand
Right up to his face.

Mummy rubs on sun cream
And says, "Keep your hats on!"
She hands out the sandwiches,
Some of which Billy sat on.

Mummy feeds Billy
And Daddy helps feed Molly,
Billy feeds squeaky moose
And Ella feeds her dolly.

Then it's time for ice cream,
A yummy cone for Stan,
And sticky orange lollies,
All melting from the van.

Dripping over fingers,
Drooling down our faces,
Mummy gets the wipes out
And cleans our sticky places.

Mummy hates mess,
It really makes her mad,
She always wipes everything,
She even wipes Dad!

And then lunch is over,
Each has had their share,
Billy's eaten pebbles
But no one seems to care.

The funfair awaits us
With its music, sounds and sights,
People screaming, horns blaring
and loads of flashing lights.

There's a carousel and dodgems,
A spooky fortune-teller,
A helter-skelter and ghost train
And a ride called 'Inter Stellar'.

There are doughnuts and candyfloss,
Sweet treats for our tummies,
Little children going round and round
And waving at their mummies.

Dad goes on the 'Caterpillar',
A roller coaster ride,
But says he won't go on again

– he's feeling odd inside.

Mum and Stan go on the 'Slammer',
Dad can hardly look,

He takes Molly, Bill and Ella
On the little 'Babbling Brook'.

Then it's into the amusements,
There's so much to be won,

Billy's got four prizes,
The rest of
us have none!

Then we stop for hot dogs
With onions and some sauce,
And a little something for afters?
Pink candyfloss, of course!

We head back to the car park
But Billy's not too happy,
We buy him a swirling windmill
And stop to change his nappy.

Before we're out of the car park
Billy's fast asleep,
We're all tired but glowing
With the memory that we'll keep

Of our day at the seaside,
Throwing pebbles by the shore,
And next time Dad's got the day off work,
We'll all be back for more!

Notes for Teachers and Parents

- Play a game of I-Spy with the children, like Molly in the story. Say, "I spy with my little eye, something beginning with…" and pick the letter your object begins with. Discuss letter sounds with the children. We can hear that 'hat' begins with an 'h' sound. Once the children have mastered single letter sounds, try conjoined sounds. For example, 'shell' begins with an 's' but the sound it starts with is formed by an 's' and 'h' joined together to make a 'sh' sound. Also try two words at a time. For example, 'ice cream' begins with 'i' and 'c'. To make the game fun for younger children, you can adapt it to use description rather than letter sounds. For example, "I spy with my little eye something that is green and brown and has leaves". A tree!

- Plan a beach-style picnic with the children. Talk about all the things you'll need. Write a list. Encourage the children to wear their sunhats and sun glasses, talk about why they need to do this and why we wear sun block. The children can draw their favourite foods on white paper plates and lay them out around a picnic blanket. Why not get out the cool box and have a real picnic, too!

- Build a funfair using junk-modelling materials, such as cereal boxes, cardboard tubes, egg boxes, yoghurt pots and aluminium foil. The children can make the rides mentioned in the story – a carousel, dodgems, helter-skelter, ghost train and roller coaster.

- Play the seaside memory game. The first player says, "I went to the seaside and with me I took…an umbrella." The second player has to repeat the sentence, remember the first object and add another to the list. For example, "I went to the seaside and with me I took an umbrella and…a bikini." The third player has to remember the first two items and add a third, and so on. Continue until the list is so long that the children can't remember any more items.

- Encourage the children to make a seaside picture. Talk about all the things you can see at the seaside and, using pens, paints, crayons and tissue paper, make a beautiful beach collage. Use shiny paper or aluminium foil for the sea. Use real sand for the beach. Collect feathers to make seagulls. Let the children's imaginations run riot.

- Help the children to make windmills. On stiff, coloured paper, draw a square, and then make cuts from the corners to just short of the centre. Bend alternate points to the centre and fasten to a drinking straw with a split pin.

- Ask the children to paint pebbles – stones provide really nice, smooth surfaces for painting on and they are a great reminder of a day out by the sea. When they're competely dry, the painted stones can be varnished and used as paperweights.